THIS BLOOMSBURY BOOK

BELONGS TO

....

For my children
for ever,

no matter what.

Bloomsbury Publishing, London, Berlin, New York and Sydney

First published in Great Britain in 1999 by Bloomsbury Publishing Plc
36 Soho Square, London, W1D 3QY

This paperback edition first published in February 2003

Text and illustrations copyright © Debi Gliori 1999
The moral right of the author/illustrator has been asserted

A CIP catalogue record of this book is available from the British Library

ISBN 978 0 7475 6331 0

Printed in Belgium by Proost, Turnhout

17 18 19 20

www.bloomsbury.com/childrens

No Matter What

Debi Gliori

BLOOMSBURY

LONDON BERLIN NEW YORK

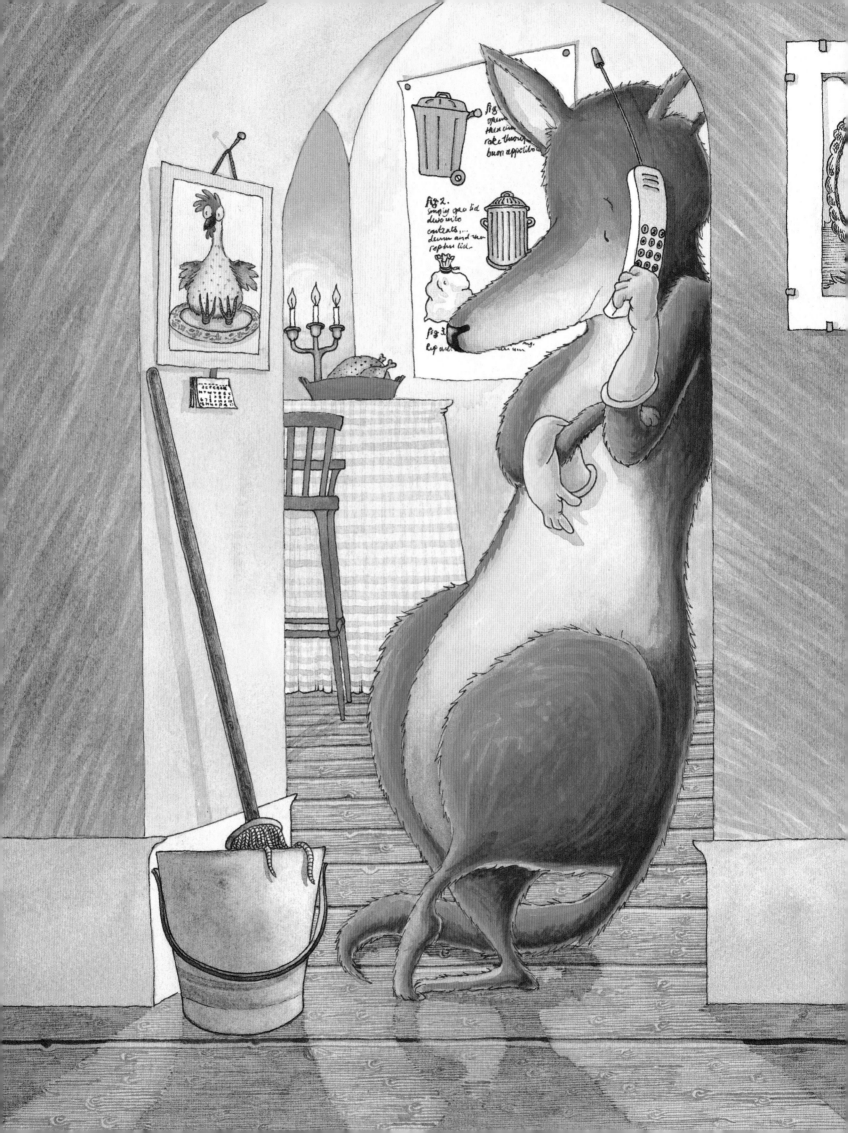

Small was feeling
grim and dark. .

Playing toss and fling and squash,
yell and scream and bang and crash.
Break and snap and bash and batter...

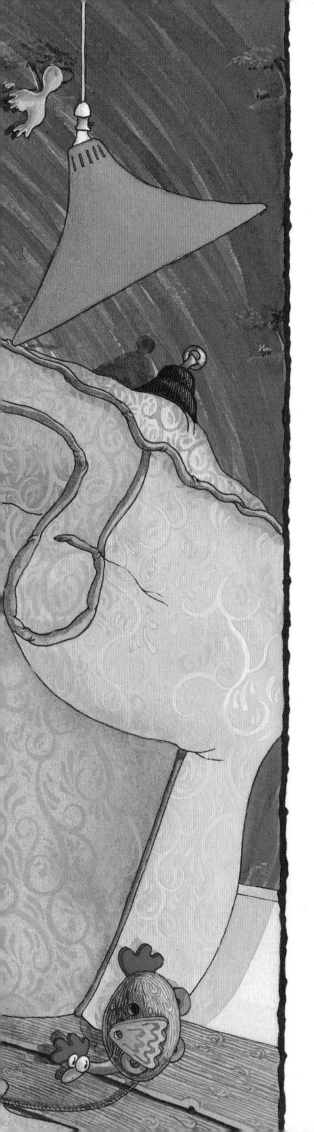

"Good grief," said Large.
"What *is* the matter?"

Small said,
"I'm a grim and grumpy
little Small
and nobody
loves me at all."

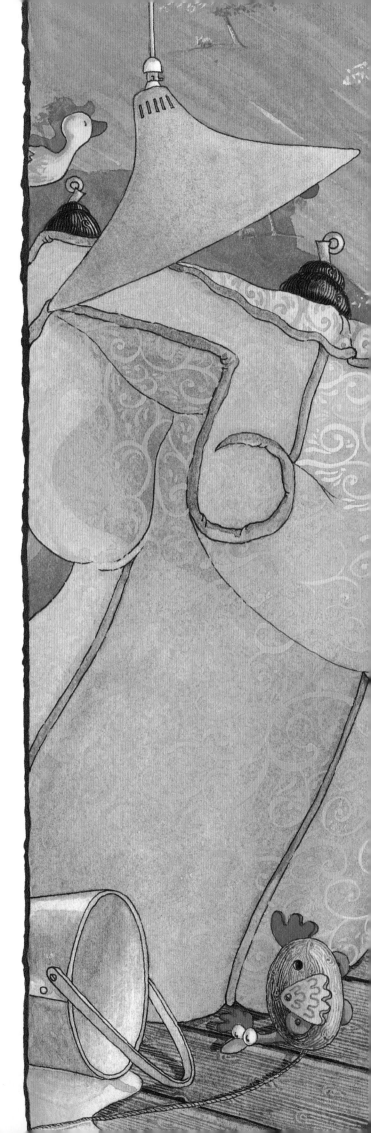

"Oh Small," said Large. "Grumpy or not,
I'll always love you no matter what."

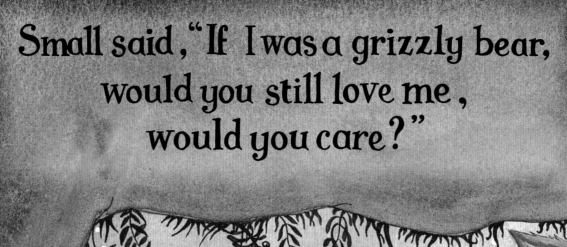

Small said, "If I was a grizzly bear,
would you still love me,
would you care?"

"Of course," said Large,
"bear or not,
I'll always love you
no matter what."

Small said, "But if I turned into a bug,

would you still love me and give me a hug?"

"Of course," said Large,
"bug or not,

I'll always love you
no matter what."

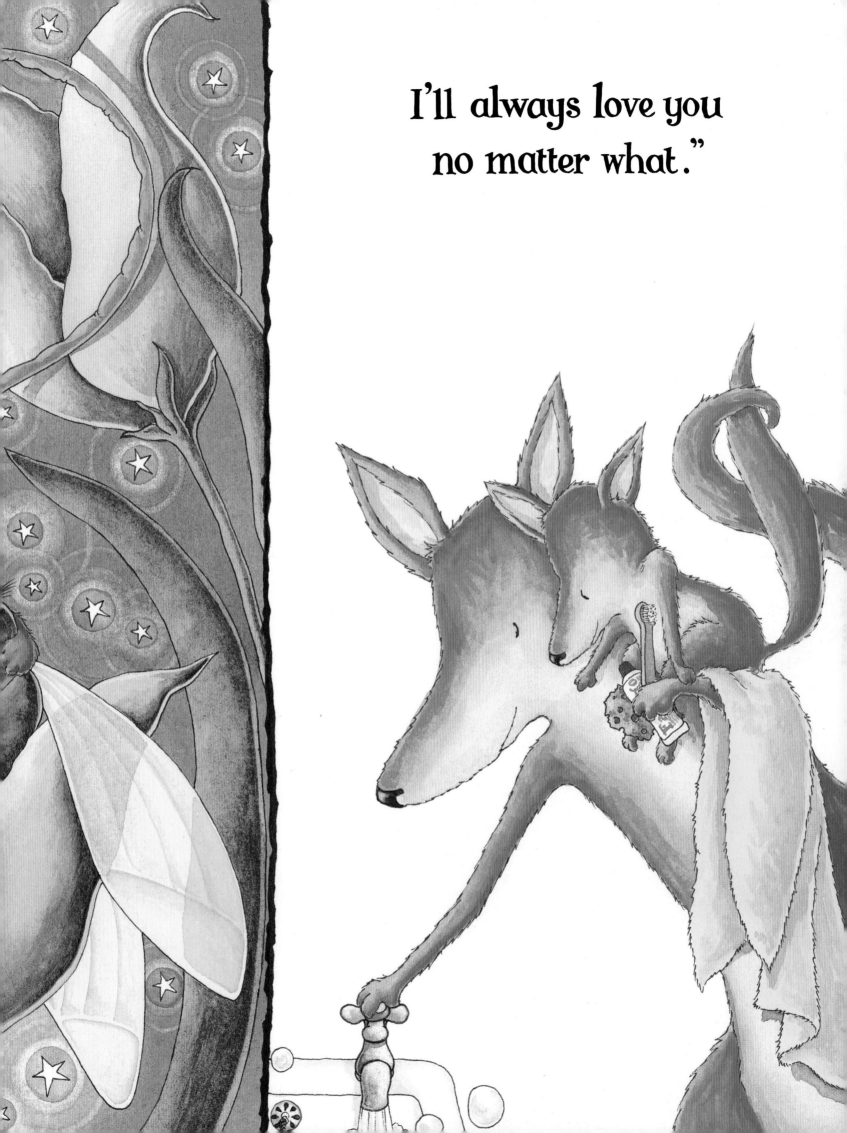

"No matter what?" said Small
and smiled.
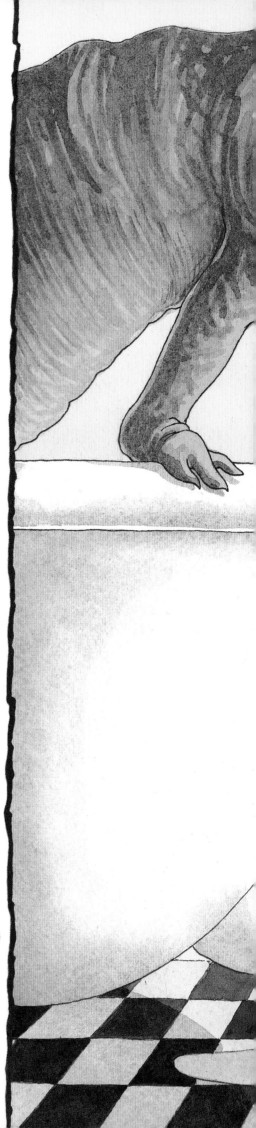

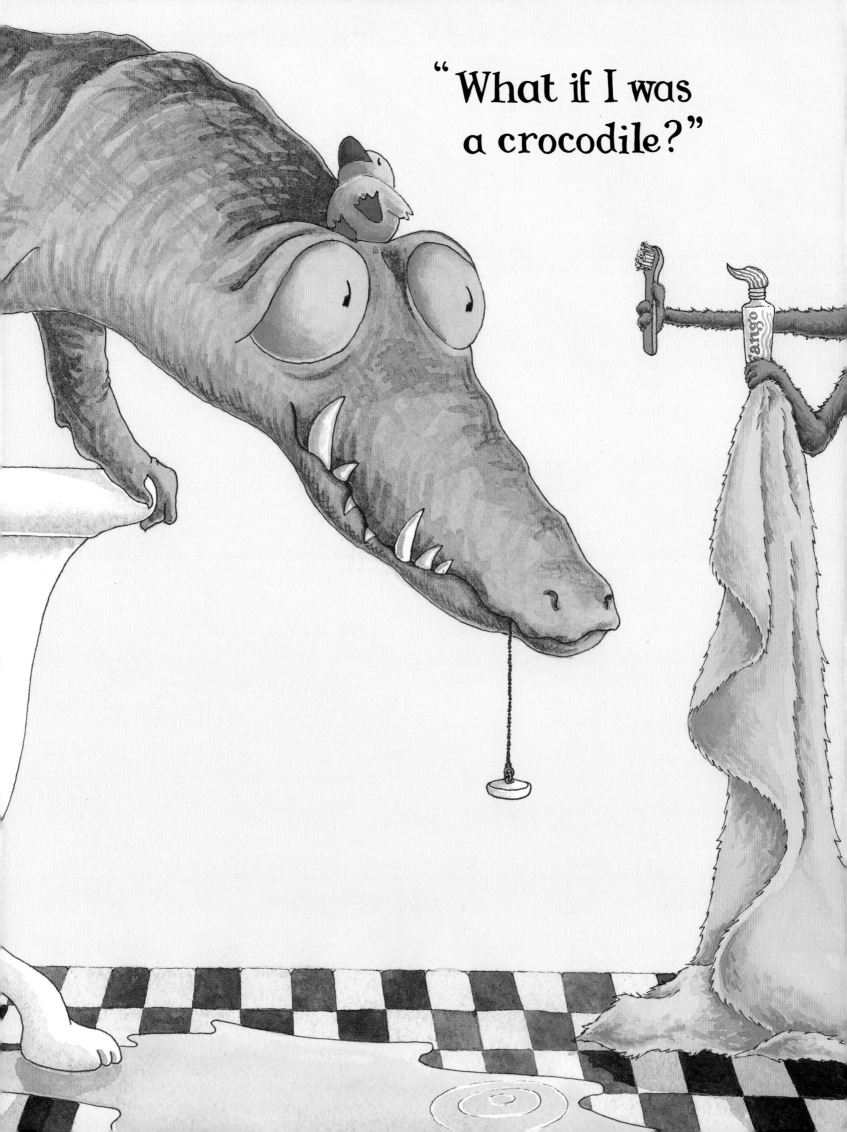

Large said, "I'd hug you close and tight, and tuck you up in bed each night."

"Does love wear out," said Small,
"does it break or bend?
Can you fix it, stick it,
does it mend?"

"Oh help," said Large, "I'm not that clever,
I just know I'll love you for ever."

Small said, "But what about when we're dead and gone, would you love me then, does love go on?"

Large held Small snug
as they looked out at the night,
at the moon in the dark,
and the stars shining bright.
"Small, look at the stars ~
how they shine and glow,
but some of those stars died
a long time ago."

"Still they shine in the evening skies
love, like starlight, never dies."

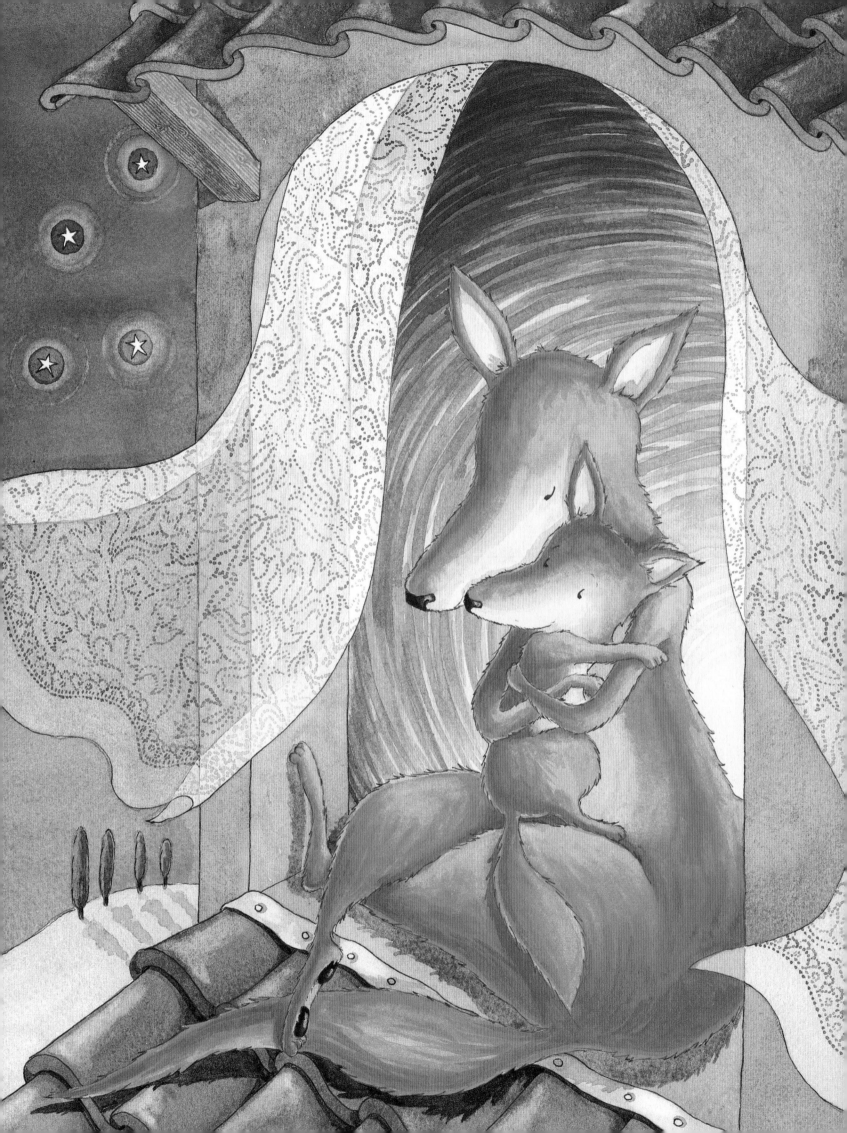

More magical moments to share, from Debi Gliori . . .

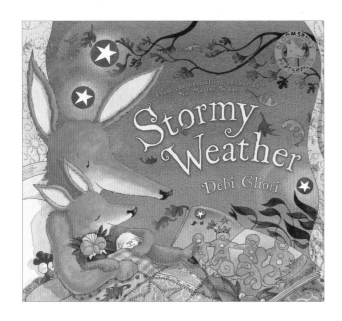

'Soothing bedtime read'
The Times

'Debi Gliori is a superb artist'
Independent